Bucky's
Journey Through
The Badger State

Aimee Aryal

Illustrated by John E Boylan

www.mascotbooks.com

Bucky Badger was enjoying a relaxing summer on the campus of the University of Wisconsin. With football season fast approaching, Bucky decided to take one last summer vacation. He thought it would be great fun to take a journey throughout the State of Wisconsin, where he could see many interesting places and make new friends along the way.

Before hitting the road, Bucky stopped at
Bascom Hall and Camp Randall Stadium
to tell his friends about his vacation plans.
His friends said, "Goodbye, Bucky! Have
a great trip!" Bucky packed his things,
hopped into the Bucky Mobile,
and was on his way!

Bucky's first stop was right in the heart of Madison. First, he went for a sail on Lake Monona. He enjoyed dressing up as a sailor! Several Wisconsin fans saw him and called, "Hello, Bucky! Smooth sailing!"

The Capitol Building was first built in 1837 and was finally completed in 1917.

After he returned to dry land, Bucky stopped at the Wisconsin State Capitol. Bucky was impressed by the beautiful Capitol building. Badger fans were happy to see the friendly mascot and they cheered, "Hello, Bucky! Go, Badgers!"

Old World Wisconsin is made up of Danish, German, Finnish, Norwegian, Polish and African-American settlements.

Bucky drove to Old World Wisconsin, where he learned what life was like in Wisconsin long ago. The mascot even dressed like a pioneer. Bucky especially enjoyed playing games with young Badger fans. "Keep that hoop rolling, Bucky," the children called.

Bucky worked in the field, guiding a horse-drawn plow. The horse neighed, "Hello, Bucky!" Once he was done with plowing, Bucky jumped on a stagecoach and drove it around, waving to people as he passed by. Bucky's fans cheered, "Go, Badgers!"

Bucky's next stop was Milwaukee, Wisconsin's largest city. He stopped by City Hall, where he organized a Wisconsin Badgers pep rally. With Bucky leading, fans cheered, "On Wisconsin!"

Bucky went to the beautiful Milwaukee Art Museum and admired many pieces of fine art. Outside the museum, fans cheered, "Hello, Bucky!"

Next up, was a trip to Miller Park to watch a Brewers baseball game. The players were happy to see Bucky at the game and they said, "Thanks for rooting us on, Bucky!"

Miller Park, the Milwaukee Brewers' home field was opened on April 6, 2001.

Bucky was ready to experience life on a modern-day Wisconsin farm. He wore overalls and drove a tractor around the fields. The family dog chased after the mascot, barking, "Go, Badgers!"

There are more cows than people in Calumet County, Wisconsin.

Since Bucky lived in the Cheese State, he wanted to see where his favorite food came from, so he visited a dairy farm. He even learned how to milk a cow! The cow mooed, "Hello, Bucky!"

Bucky knew that milk was an important ingredient for making cheese, but he wanted to learn more about Wisconsin's famous food product.

To learn more, Bucky stopped at a cheese factory! Bucky joined the assembly line and helped to make delicious blocks of cheddar cheese. The workers were excited to have a famous celebrity working alongside them. "Hello, Bucky! Welcome to the factory!" they said. As he worked, Bucky thought about all the ways he loved to eat cheese. Yummy!

The state of Wisconsin produces
25% of all cheese in the U.S.,
more than any other state.

After working so hard, Bucky wanted to relax a bit, so he went bass fishing on Lake Michigan with some new friends. They were all excited when Bucky caught a big one! "Way to go, Bucky! He's a beauty!" they cheered. In a worried voice, the mascot's catch said, "Hello, Bucky!"

The Algoma Pierhead lighthouse was built in 1893.

Kewaunee Pierhead lighthouse was built in 1891.

Bucky was interested in seeing some of the lighthouses along Lake Michigan and learning about their history. The mascot stopped at Algoma and Kewaunee lighthouses. He climbed to the top and enjoyed spectacular views of Lake Michigan. At every stop, people noticed the mascot and cheered, "Hello, Bucky!"

Fans of the Green Bay Packers are known as "Cheese Heads" because of the cheese hats they wear to Packers games.

Bucky knew that no trip around the state of Wisconsin was complete without a stop in Green Bay. He drove the Bucky Mobile to Lambeau Field, home of the Green Bay Packers. He wore a special "cheese head" hat and joined Packers fans for a tour of the historic stadium. They all ate bratwursts and talked about the upcoming season.

Bucky ventured into the Packers' locker room and got a chance to meet the team's star quarterback! Bucky was a little nervous about meeting his football hero, but the star player put him at ease by saying, "Welcome to Green Bay, Bucky! Go, Badgers!"

> *The famous sea caves of Squaw Bay are only accessible by boat during the summer.*

Bucky was enjoying his trip, but he wanted to see more of the state's natural beauty, so he took a canoe on to Lake Superior and paddled along the Apostle Island National Lakeshore. He visited the Squaw Bay Sea Caves and marveled at how stunningly beautiful they were!

After seeing such natural beauty, Bucky was ready to see another lighthouse. He stopped at the Sand Island lighthouse on the shores of Lake Superior. The lighthouse keeper saw Bucky coming and offered to show him the observation tower at the top. Bucky loved the great view!

The annual Lumberjack World Championships are held every July in Hayward, Wisconsin.

Bucky's next stop was the Lumberjack World Championships in Hayward, Wisconsin. Bucky decided to enter the competition! He was the last one standing for the log-rolling competition. Badger fans cheered, "Nice rolling, Bucky!"

Next up was a sawing contest. With all his might, Bucky sawed through a thick tree trunk. Bucky could saw so fast, the blade was just a blur! "Go, Bucky, go!" the crowd chanted!

After several lumberjacking events, Bucky finished in first place and won the championship!

The St. Croix River is 164 miles long and is a tributary of the Mississippi River.

Bucky's next adventure was canoeing on the St. Croix River.

That evening, Bucky set up camp along the river with some friends. They roasted s'mores and swapped stories. Everyone was fascinated about Bucky's journey all over Wisconsin. As he rested in his sleeping bag, Bucky thought about what a beautiful state Wisconsin was.

Having traveled all over the entire Badger State, Bucky finally made it back to Madison and the University of Wisconsin. What a great vacation it had been! All his fans were thrilled at his return and cheered, "Hello, Bucky! Welcome home!"

At last back in his own room, Bucky thought about all the interesting place he visited and the great friends he made along the way. He crawled into his own bed and fell fast asleep.

Good night, Bucky!

Washburn

Ashland

Hayward

Grantsburg

Shell Lake

Balsam Lake

Barron

Ladysmith

Hudson

Chippewa Falls

Menomonie

Eau Claire

Ellsworth

Durand

Neillsville

Whitehall

94

Alma

Black Rive

Sparta

90

La Crosse

Viroqua

Prairie
du Chien

Lancas

Bucky's
Journey Through
The Badger State

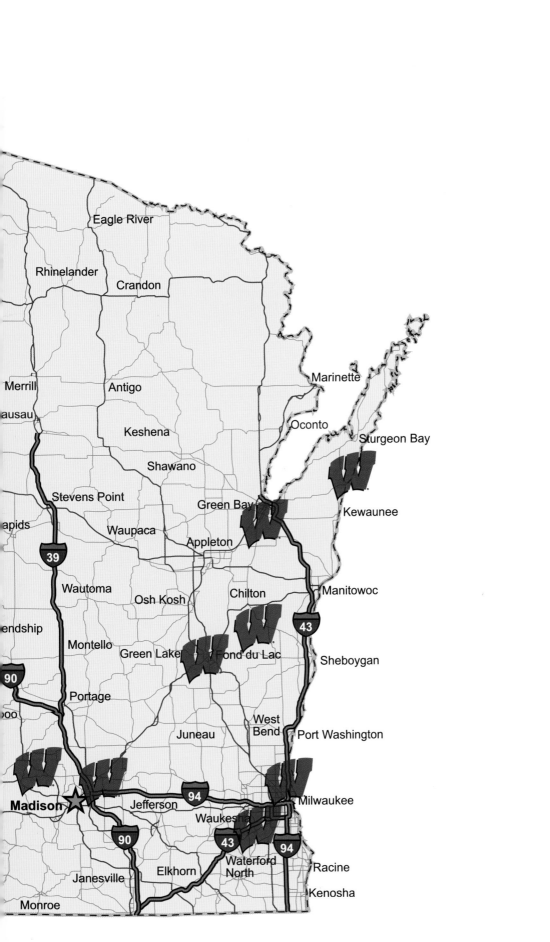

For Anna and Maya. ~ Aimee Aryal

For my Parents, John & Jacqueline Boylan ~ John E Boylan

For more information about our products,
please visit us online at www.mascotbooks.com.

For more information, please contact Mascot Books,
P.O. Box 220157, Chantilly, VA 20153-0157

UNIVERSITY OF WISCONSIN, WISCONSIN, UW, W,
UNIVERSITY OF WISCONSIN BADGERS, BADGERS, BADGER,
WISCONSIN BADGERS, BUCKY BADGER, BUCKY, KOHL CENTER and
CAMP RANDALL STADIUM are trademarks or registered trademarks of
The University of Wisconsin and are used under license.

ISBN: 1-934878-14-6

Printed in the United States.

www.mascotbooks.com

Title List

Major League Baseball

Boston Red Sox	Hello, *Wally*!	Jerry Remy
Boston Red Sox	*Wally The Green Monster And His Journey Through Red Sox Nation*!	Jerry Remy
Boston Red Sox	Coast to Coast with *Wally The Green Monster*	Jerry Remy
Boston Red Sox	A Season with *Wally The Green Monster*	Jerry Remy
Colorado Rockies	Hello, *Dinger*!	Aimee Aryal
Detroit Tigers	Hello, *Paws*!	Aimee Aryal
New York Yankees	Let's Go, *Yankees*!	Yogi Berra
New York Yankees	*Yankees Town*	Aimee Aryal
New York Mets	Hello, *Mr. Met*!	Rusty Staub
New York Mets	*Mr. Met* and his Journey Through the Big Apple	Aimee Aryal
St. Louis Cardinals	Hello, *Fredbird*!	Ozzie Smith
Philadelphia Phillies	Hello, *Phillie Phanatic*!	Aimee Aryal
Chicago Cubs	Let's Go, *Cubs*!	Aimee Aryal
Chicago White Sox	Let's Go, *White Sox*!	Aimee Aryal
Cleveland Indians	Hello, *Slider*!	Bob Feller
Seattle Mariners	Hello, *Mariner Moose*!	Aimee Aryal
Washington Nationals	Hello, *Screech*!	Aimee Aryal
Milwaukee Brewers	Hello, *Bernie Brewer*!	Aimee Aryal

College

Alabama	Hello, Big Al!	Aimee Aryal
Alabama	Roll Tide!	Ken Stabler
Alabama	Big Al's Journey Through the Yellowhammer State	Aimee Aryal
Arizona	Hello, Wilbur!	Lute Olson
Arkansas	Hello, Big Red!	Aimee Aryal
Arkansas	Big Red's Journey Through the Razorback State	Aimee Aryal
Auburn	Hello, Aubie!	Aimee Aryal
Auburn	War Eagle!	Pat Dye
Auburn	Aubie's Journey Through the Yellowhammer State	Aimee Aryal
Boston College	Hello, Baldwin!	Aimee Aryal
Brigham Young	Hello, Cosmo!	LaVell Edwards
Cal - Berkeley	Hello, Oski!	Aimee Aryal
Clemson	Hello, Tiger!	Aimee Aryal
Clemson	Tiger's Journey Through the Palmetto State	Aimee Aryal
Colorado	Hello, Ralphie!	Aimee Aryal
Connecticut	Hello, Jonathan!	Aimee Aryal
Duke	Hello, Blue Devil!	Aimee Aryal
Florida	Hello, Albert!	Aimee Aryal
Florida State	Let's Go, 'Noles!	Aimee Aryal
Georgia	Hello, Hairy Dawg!	Aimee Aryal
Georgia	How 'Bout Them Dawgs!	Aimee Aryal
Georgia	Hairy Dawg's Journey Through the Peach State	Vince Dooley
Georgia Tech	Hello, Buzz!	Aimee Aryal
Gonzaga	Spike, The Gonzaga Bulldog	Mike Pringle
Illinois	Let's Go, Illini!	Aimee Aryal
Indiana	Let's Go, Hoosiers!	Aimee Aryal
Iowa	Hello, Herky!	Aimee Aryal
Iowa State	Hello, Cy!	Aimee Aryal
James Madison	Hello, Duke Dog!	Amy DeLashmutt
Kansas	Hello, Big Jay!	Aimee Aryal
Kansas State	Hello, Willie!	Aimee Aryal
Kentucky	Hello, Wildcat!	Dan Walter
LSU	Hello, Mike!	Aimee Aryal
LSU	Mike's Journey Through the Bayou State	Aimee Aryal
Maryland	Hello, Testudo!	Aimee Aryal
Michigan	Let's Go, Blue!	Aimee Aryal
Michigan State	Hello, Sparty!	Aimee Aryal
Minnesota	Hello, Goldy!	Aimee Aryal
Mississippi	Hello, Colonel Rebel!	Aimee Aryal
Mississippi State	Hello, Bully!	Aimee Aryal

Pro Football

Carolina Panthers	Let's Go, Panthers!	Aimee Aryal
Chicago Bears	Let's Go, Bears!	Aimee Aryal
Dallas Cowboys	How 'Bout Them Cowboys!	Aimee Aryal
Green Bay Packers	Go, Pack, Go!	Aimee Aryal
Kansas City Chiefs	Let's Go, Chiefs!	Aimee Aryal
Minnesota Vikings	Let's Go, Vikings!	Aimee Aryal
New York Giants	Let's Go, Giants!	Aimee Aryal
New York Jets	J-E-T-S! Jets, Jets, Jets!	Aimee Aryal
New England Patriots	Let's Go, Patriots!	Aimee Aryal
Pittsburgh Steelers	Here We Go Steelers!	Aimee Aryal
Seattle Seahawks	Let's Go, Seahawks!	Aimee Aryal
Washington Redskins	Hail To The Redskins!	Aimee Aryal

Basketball

Dallas Mavericks	Let's Go, Mavs!	Mark Cuban
Boston Celtics	Let's Go, Celtics!	Aimee Aryal

Other

Kentucky Derby	White Diamond Runs For The Roses	Aimee Aryal
Marine Corps Marathon	Run, Miles, Run!	Aimee Aryal

Missouri	Hello, Truman!	Aimee Aryal
Nebraska	Hello, Herbie Husker!	Todd Donoho
North Carolina	Hello, Rameses!	Aimee Aryal
North Carolina	Rameses' Journey Through the Tar Heel State	Aimee Aryal
North Carolina St.	Hello, Mr. Wuf!	Aimee Aryal
North Carolina St.	Mr. Wuf's Journey Through North Carolina	Aimee Aryal
Notre Dame	Let's Go, Irish!	Aimee Aryal
Ohio State	Hello, Brutus!	Aimee Aryal
Ohio State	Brutus' Journey	Aimee Aryal
Oklahoma	Let's Go, Sooners!	Aimee Aryal
Oklahoma State	Hello, Pistol Pete!	Aimee Aryal
Oregon	Go Ducks!	Aimee Aryal
Oregon State	Hello, Benny the Beaver!	Aimee Aryal
Penn State	Hello, Nittany Lion!	Aimee Aryal
Penn State	We Are Penn State!	Joe Paterno
Purdue	Hello, Purdue Pete!	Aimee Aryal
Rutgers	Hello, Scarlet Knight!	Aimee Aryal
South Carolina	Hello, Cocky!	Aimee Aryal
South Carolina	Cocky's Journey Through the Palmetto State	Aimee Aryal
So. California	Hello, Tommy Trojan!	Aimee Aryal
Syracuse	Hello, Otto!	Aimee Aryal
Tennessee	Hello, Smokey!	Aimee Aryal
Tennessee	Smokey's Journey Through the Volunteer State	Aimee Aryal
Texas	Hello, Hook 'Em!	Aimee Aryal
Texas	Hook 'Em's Journey Through the Lone Star State	Aimee Aryal
Texas A & M	Howdy, Reveille!	Aimee Aryal
Texas A & M	Reveille's Journey Through the Lone Star State	Aimee Aryal
Texas Tech	Hello, Masked Rider!	Aimee Aryal
UCLA	Hello, Joe Bruin!	Aimee Aryal
Virginia	Hello, CavMan!	Aimee Aryal
Virginia Tech	Hello, Hokie Bird!	Aimee Aryal
Virginia Tech	Yea, It's Hokie Game Day!	Frank Beamer
Virginia Tech	Hokie Bird's Journey Through Virginia	Aimee Aryal
Wake Forest	Hello, Demon Deacon!	Aimee Aryal
Washington	Hello, Harry the Husky!	Aimee Aryal
Washington State	Hello, Butch!	Aimee Aryal
West Virginia	Hello, Mountaineer!	Aimee Aryal
Wisconsin	Hello, Bucky!	Aimee Aryal
Wisconsin	Bucky's Journey Through the Badger State	Aimee Aryal

Order online at **mascotbooks.com** using promo code " **free**" to receive **FREE SHIPPING!**

More great titles coming soon!

info@mascotbooks.com

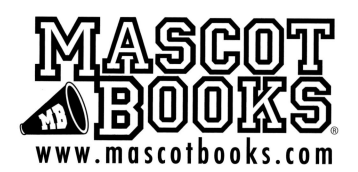
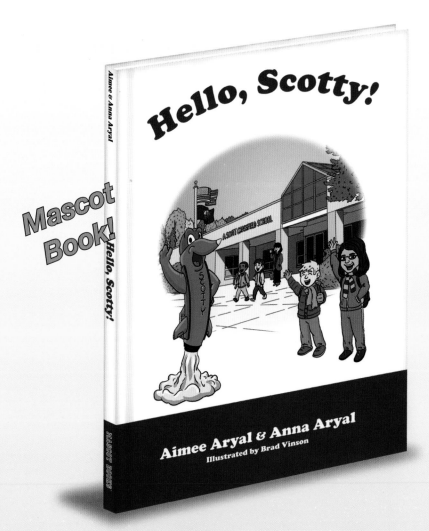

Let Mascot Books create a customized children's book for your school or team!

Here's how our fundraisers work ...

- Mascot Books creates a customized children's book with content specific to your school. When parents buy your school's book, your organization earns cash!

- When parents buy any of Mascot Books' college or professional team books, your organization earns more cash!

- We also offer options for a customized plush, apparel, and even mascot costumes!

Mascot Costumes!

Dougie the Dragon

Mascot T-Shirts!

Proud to be a Vincent Elementary Duck!

Vinny the Duck

Mascot Plush!

Lulu the Ladybug

For more information about the most innovative fundraiser on the market, contact us at info@mascotbooks.com.